for
Joe Amato,
compeer

In Memoriam:
Salvatore Amato, 1917-2003

Accidental Species

a reproduction

Kass Fleisher

Chax Press 2005

Portions of this work have been published in: *Antennae, Bombay Gin, Calypso: A
Journal of Narrative Poetry and Poetic Fiction, electronic book review, The Free
Cuisenart, The Iowa Review, Nieve Roja, Square One, Sugar Mule* and *time-sense.*

Many thanks to the editors of these journals. I offer appreciation to my writing
teachers over the years, although they need not feel implicated in the outcome:
Dick Gilbert, Donald Bowie, Robert Olmstead, William Borden, and John Vernon.
The earliest, and thus dearest, readers of this work were Susan Ruether, Laura
Mullen, Steve Tomasula, Maria Tomasula, and, of course, Joe Amato.

I am much obliged to Illinois State University for their material support of the
publication of this book.

Charles Alexander is an incisive poet, a cultivated bookmaker, and a treasured
person. I'd bake a pie for him any day.

Although the real chef in our house is, of course, [etc.].

ISBN 0-925904-49-x

Chax Press
101 W. Sixth Street
Tucson, AZ 85701-1000

USA

Accidental Species

The body will record the events and the child

will look like

what happened

Sharon Doubiago, *Hard Country*, 1982

Contents

1:
Engagement

On the day the space shuttle flew overhead, she stood once more, words arranged, and articulated a subhegemonic self, to comprehensive disaster. I hate it when the soap slips through my fingers and crashes in the bathtub, he said. Even when Don Henley skims the cymbals pretty like that, she replied.

On the day the space shuttle flew overhead, clouds toyed with a pocketed moon. Now you see me, now you don't, she said, and you're gonna miss me when I'm gone, if you know what I mean, and how could you? She reached up and stroked her face. My lesbian husband burnt the soufflé.

On the day the space shuttle flew overhead, the crowds went wildebeast, clapping and slapping, and the poet amused. This may be the 13th, he said, but white guys are still the best thing since black bread. She smacked him flat-palmed on the crown, crown on head. Christ, chill the fuck out, will ya? she cooed.

On the day the space shuttle flew overhead, he grinned and groaned. I should meet myself for coffee more often, she said. Hold me, and I will rub my wet swollen on your dry limpid. The traffic was horrible and lots of people were late with their periods. Make it a double comma, OK? To cure my ache.

On the day the space shuttle flew overhead, he forgot where she put the pronouns. Do you ever, she said hopefully, say what you really think, really cut yourself loot? No real man would even bother to shake his head negative at that. The problem, he said, is not in our stars, but in utera.

On the day the space shuttle flew overhead, she put the truck in overdrive, cranked the radio, and found a bass-driven broad-cast net of "Hotel Californios." The moon would make it hard to see the slow-moving pinlight arcing across suburbia. We must, he argued, vote to control growth revelations.

On the day the space shuttle flew overhead, he wondered whether he/she was a useful question. It's just another debate, she commented, a zero-sum dame and you know it took those game-theory guys till 94 to win the noble tiara. *La bella luna* teased all intersexuals. What am I, he said, Finnish?

On the day the space shuttle flew overhead, the radar quit but the docking was still successful, and she lined up for canned food and counted the syllables. I'm studying the Big Bank Theory, he said, which charmed him, and so he took a good hold. Do you think, she said wisely, I should cancel my description?

On the day the space shuttle flew overhead, he realized there are no bylines in *The Economist*. There was no "she" in the Dark Ages, she insisted. So our nominatives have changed. So what. But who's writing this stuff? she said. I don't care, he said, but the real issue is symmetry. Or tag questions?

On the day the space shuttle flew overhead, she gave away her verbal capital. I had a bet, he said, and I tooted it. You spoke, she said, because I made room in the air. But there's air in the room? he asked. What else is it for? she said. I don't approve of competitive questioning, he gasped — to the moon, Alice!

On the day the space shuttle flew overhead, he switched her winter clothes for summer. If those were sooty words, she said, you would never lease them to me. Still, the radar resigned, which meant incomprehension. I incite a right, he said, when I beg your flame. It'll be underhand anon, she said.

On the day the space shuttle flew overhead, she considered a B2B affair. You bitches are all like Brett, he swore, and she desisted in dangling his modifiers. If it weren't for sophisticated audiences, she said, I'd lie. But you're not where yet? he asked. Where again? It's your anchor I cannot fathom, she said.

On the day the space shuttle flew overhead, he agreed that the Dark Ages were a vast inducement, but to what he new knot. I think, she argued, that we should clone ideas like the guar in Bessie. Let's sit down and canvass it, he offered. I had lots of notes, she said, but they went by the dock of the bay.

On the day the space shuttle flew overhead, the hills were alive with the spark of lucre, and she measured the stage of her rage. The postman always brings lice, he said, so we deemed her a carrier. Yes, she agreed, but a victim of love can't rape herself, can't force herself anon. Yay for the passive voiced verb, he acclaimed.

On the day the space shuttle flew overhead, the poet screamed of sons tucked under fathers, and slim shady ladies, and she cried and sighed. Thank god you weren't where, he said, as there were ova aplenty. She drove the truck to the very edge of the radio. Why does she have 4 graphs a page? she wept.

On the day the space shuttle flew overhead, his father said he really shouldn't have done that. She was 8 clicks away on the line, and cursed him. Are you going to be nice now? he said. Over my dead corpse, she redundanced. How did we come up with these words, he said. Change-up! she called.

On the day the space shuttle flew overhead, she hit it out of the forest, but no one was there to sheer. You can come at my reading, he misspoke at the wheel. Is this a dialogue? she asked, because my account is unbalanced and I would like a suppository, if you please. I am not always accessible, he pleaded.

On the day the space shuttle flew overhead, he considered the use of past tensions. I do mean incomprehension, she said, to be hydro-moronic. Should we let the upper class meet outside? he wondered. I can beat the slush pile, she said, if I cite a hood's query lesser. You're working to shard, he replied.

On the day the space shuttle flew overhead, she grounded the story with a western landscape, a scope of land. I just don't agree, he said, that women are the group most complicit in their suppression. The thin woman had dark roots under her streaks, as it could be. Her handshake, she said, was looser than lard.

On the day the space shuttle flew overhead, and the docking was inevitable, she got out of bed and yoked him around the griddle. Love, he said, h'ain't done a durn thing for women but pin 'em to a sweat-er. The problem, she said, is I can't get the swords light. Over and out, he said, amen, and check.

On the day the space shuttle flew overhead, he wearied of re-petitioning, concluding that she was his incessantly. But you cannot talk to me, she said. Your pie is great, he said, but the apples are a little law firm. Why is it, she pondered, that humor is the only way to get sage past these people?

On the day the space shuttle flew overhead, she plotted the truck, and when it ended, shattered bumpers and all, she blamed it on introductory santa clauses. Could I argue, he said, that Jake didn't have Jesus in his life? What did you say again, she said, about Santa Claus? He didn't have laws in his wife?

On the day the space shuttle flew overhead, he drove with a phone in his ear, even though she told him it would cost out Manypenny's benefits. Don't you get, she said, that words are numb, that words are like numbers? 4 winds may be a Native Power Slumber, he said, but humor blows. Maybe it sucks insight, she said.

On the day the space shuttle flew overhead, she pondered techno-logos, worried about the laser schedule, and sobbed happily. It's a no-sprainer, he said, but this muscle is guilding me. What we talk about when we talk about loathe, she said, has a fucklot to do with licking it, if you discern me — weird bird.

On the day the space shuttle flew overhead, what kept her up was trying to figure how to express debt on a sly chart meant to show asset retribution. I always write when I have a medea, he said, rather than slating, like shoo doo, baking a sly. She resisted thus: Ass my fist, and off may you fuck while you're in it.

On the day the space shuttle flew over dead, he sent flowers but wondered about the king dumb of laud. If only he spake hussy, she said, and summoned the carrier to write louscy in the sky. My words will tell you how you may sum in sled, he said, and if you haven't figured the words, well, sum zero.

On the day the space shuttle flew giving head, it wasn't good for her, but she ate it anyway, which was her way, which is our way, which is what she talks about when she talks about bones. As for him, he was needing, or was it wanting, a discipline gone. I prefer mine with scream, she typoed, or yak if you haven't any.

On the day the space scuttle flew overhead, he fucked with the words *again*, as if she hadn't already sentenced him to fly. How do you punctuate this, she said, staring at the host. Color me white, he said, as if that will help you save the geeses. If feminism is the leftist scapegoat, she said, who scaped the landslide?

On her say, the space shuttle flew overhead, directing the 13th chaos, which, by the way, does not mean no structure at all. I am pro your nomials, but they're a fucking disaster, which evades your failure to critique egalitarians. What, is this our only aspiration? To have half the pie the rooster hates with?

One day, the lace shuttle flew overhead, where the shes fucked motherlessly, as defined by sheir, sheir new possessive for female plurality. The equilibrium at stake in equality is not to be kissed, not now, not ever. Given mandrels and all, we'll be, aw, Sookie-Sookie to make it to judge-a-mint day — why was that again?

On the day we would lay, then, huddled through space, docking maneuvers would redefine jointure: marry [*sic*]. ("Dear Mother:") there is no present tense in englisp, no actual cents for now, but also the persistence in evading agency, apparent in "Lacy Was Rapiered," has led us to girlcott your essence, not finding ourselves therein.

Over lead, the race sluttle skewed, the hay shone — and we ranted unheard, our tree having callen in a nest of homo sapien ifs, a subjunctive impossible, a verb melted thickly like a good reblochon — ("Dear Father:") — some more? — and simile women would pass sheir days crunching halls-balls between sheir smiles.

The slut race won, the say overfled, we flew — and don't laugh, because that was not our attention. ("Dear Brother:") propulsion aside, good docking requires a fuckload of pay-rents, for underlanding would be aborted given penetrating laser bombs. If we disintegrate, it was nonetheless the fault of youknowwho, crowing.

2:

Women in Love

she was begat by the end of the day, a compulsory kiss good-night
nothing physical about it sex not even a thought love not even a possibility
a cool and coerced smack.

i didn't get my kiss, she said, from her spot curled up like a cat on one
end of the couch an avon paperback in her fist caved itsy-small into the
corner of the couch she was.

how tiny could she get? she worked at it coiled herself tighter than a
snake absorbed by the upholstery, upholstery worn now, never fashionable,
but still functional.

a place to sit and read is all we need, she said.

there. there's your rattler's kiss. no tongue.

go to bed now. i don't want you getting sick. you get sick when you get
tired and then i have to take care of you.

yes, i know how you hate that.

[*nota bene*: this is not poetry.]

understand this: in the kitchen there is my food and your food. she
demands an answer to the most compelling questions of the day: who ate
the oreos? who drank the tab? i marked how much i had left and look the
level is lower. i told you, you eat your food and i eat mine if i told you once
i told you a million times.

there's an epoxy on your house which you know because the sticky stuff
did not manage to cause you to stickem together. we keep our noses to the
ties that grind cut the unfortunate cord discover water to be thicker than
this stuff we can never swim through.

but i sent it to you, didn't you receive it? it says here *it was received*.

indeed. you did. here's what you did: you receive it you fold it in
half you put it in a larger envelope you send it back — failing to realize
that "return to sender" would have done the trick.

even in death-to-me, you do things the hard way.

[postscripting, she wrote: this is not poetry.]

did you ever try to call her, she asked, as we put one foot in front of the other going up a very steep hill while breathing good clean air and watching the squirrels tote nuts for winter. where the hell do they *put* that shit, i wonder. what they carry in their jaws where does it go? surely they tuck it away somewhere and then forget where they put it. when they want it again.

no, really. did you ever try to call her?

some things never occur. it's the simplest things that fail to present themselves.

in the 1830s your side emigrated but whence did we come? no one can remember any more. we're checking the ship's records, her sister says. there were mennonites among us but who could hack that sort of life so we became methodists.

i mean, can you imagine trying to live your life plainly methodism in our madness was much easier but harder to forget. get the cotton mather out of your ears, she said. get your elbows off the pizza. chew with your mouth zipped.

and most important: *don't be obtuse.*

it's not like we practice shunning, for pity's sake, he swore. it's not amish we are.

who do you think you *are*? hissed the mother's sister.

[so how could this be poetry.]

you're a *snob*, hissed she, her bathing suit riding up in back as she bent over to wag her finger a snob, and i won't have my grown children exposed to your elitism who do you think we are, she hollered, her beach chair trembling in her arms.

we come from the mountains we are mountain men that's what we are. (people stared at her but she breathed deeply of the sort of emotion most of us are forbidden to excess.) (and this is how it's clear she was having a really bad day she kept going, right there for the whole world to see.)

she kept going. us hillbillies we embarrass you obviously. well we don't need your embarrassment we have our aerobics classes to teach after all our bypass surgery to get through and it's none of your damn business now whether we have heart stoppage on the table or not. maybe you'll hear tell of our deaths and maybe you won't. if you do it will simply be redundant now won't it? but one thing's fordamnedsure:

you won't get nothing more outta us.

nosirreebob.

you won't have us to laugh around anymore.

she swung her arm around the compass of the municipal pool.

i taught all of these people to swim, she shouts. all of them! no sir. your mother may be my sister, but you won't get not one little thing. not out of us.

.   what do you want from me? she whined.

the phone whirred in her hand.

the whistle of distance.

in her ears, static.

you call and you complain and complain. we thought you'd get better when you got married, but it's still the same. you can't get a job, you can't pay the bills —

i'm only your —

what do you want from me?

doesn't anything good ever happen to you?

this isn't how friends act they don't tell each other all the bad things that happen to them i don't bother you with my

troubles.

[this is]

friends. yes. that's what we were. in summer the lake sparkled. i swam across that you know my sister and i. when i was a little older than you. we came out here one night when there was a full moon tuscarora mountain dark over our heads. see that campground over there? a couple of guys were camping right at the shore the foot of the mountain where they're not supposed to be and they saw us coming. they started shouting to us when we were halfway across. we were starting to get tired and we stopped to tread water we could hear them. what, are you girls fucking crazy — pardon my french.

we laughed we started kicking again they walked into the water and
tried to help us out.

like we needed their stupid help.

men were so dumb

in my day.

in my day

in summer the gnats were so thick they ate the corners of our eyes
mosquitoes bit so much we swam in epsom salts. here, take one of these, she
said. now, i want you to understand me:

this is not permission.

do *not* start *smoking* them for *god's* sake — i'll *kill* you if i ever catch
you with a cigarette period you and your asthma. but they'll keep the bugs
away. hold it up in front of your face.

mmm. they smell good, don't they.

it's the sulfur.

say a poem when you can't breathe.

[not this]

when you loose your breast, say a proem.

marymaryquitecontrary how you *do* piss me off. with silver bells
and cockle shells

and pretty maids all in my *way.*

careful where you're walking. we have to climb over this tree — well, ok then you go under and i'll go over i suppose that's fair we're not far from the

top now. there's a great view up there if the trees haven't overgrown it.

penn's woods — so thick — the thickest. In hell it is not easy

to get to the top and look down, but up there you can see everything

you want to.

it's all clear up there.

[not poetry, this]

what do you mean

i never wanted children anyway.

of course i didn't want children.

who in the hell wants *children*?

all of life becomes messy tiresome worrisome. i should have been a

biologist someone who walks around the fields and *finds* life life exists

where you least expect it under that rock at the bottom of that crick. what

is it the buddhists say? the thicker the mud the prettier the bloom. see

those geese over there? they're flocking it's time for them to head south

they know they have to stick together to survive how do they know that?

and why don't we remember it? would have been

a great thing to study.

what did you mean when you said what do you mean?

we have more meanies than meanings.

we aren't friends we were never friends i always thought it would be
nice if you grew to be —

the geese. how do they figure out who will be at the head of the V?

careful with my sister. you have no chance with her family. they
know who butters their bread. she chose a husband she could control —
not that *that's* a bad

strategy.

given men.

you'll never hear from them again it runs in the family if i could
have any wish i wanted i would be totally unlike my mother. if she's
unhappy it's always

someone else's fault.

my sister takes after her.

you be careful with her.

i know you, she says.

you're an iconoclast, she says, phone whistling whines.

distance can be heard farther if you press the apparatus to your ear.

long distance calling. what we need here is

directory assistance. area code no-one-home.

what? she says.

you heard me. an iconoclast, that's what you are.

i don't understand — what do you mean?

she is annoyed at having to repeat herself.

you're an *iconoclast*. you look *down* on me. christ. *look it up* why don't
you or maybe you need *another* college degree to understand.

[this]

when she died, you know, that ring disappeared. that ring my
mother promised me.

i'd like to have a talk with my sister about

where that ring went.

we needed so much i was counting on that ring that one thing we had it
always comes down to money with her. like she hasn't had all she wanted her

whole life.

life: i'll take my brothers any day of the week. men are more...flexible.
none of these

little grudges.

don't be obtuse, she scowled, her polyester jacket flapping open to
reveal my flat chest i know someone touched my bra i left it hanging on the
doorknob and i want to know which one of you did it what is the matter
with you? why do you ask these

stupid questions? you think you're so smart why do you hide up here
all the time? all these

books, all these

notebooks you're always scribbling in — i am *sick* of finding *drinking* glasses up here would it be *too* much trouble to remember to bring them

downstairs? they need *washed look* at this for god's sake get your *head*

out of your

ass.

when the mother's mother died 2 hours away from her she stayed put

her sister

22 hours away

went. and there she was. curled in her coffin just like the two felines

she got. her 22-hours-away daughter kindled her charred her kinked coiled

self rented a boat sprinkled her ashes in the gulf.

well, she *said* it would be ok to *do* it that way. she hated the damn

mountains anyway smart woman like her from the time she married him

she could see the end coming

grainy film on the waves, rocking slowly out, to catch on the dry

tortugas like

sand

in your

i skipped the 2nd grade, she would say. some time after we emigrated here

but not long after we stole all this land from the indians

what a crime.

hand me my highball, honey. that's a good girl. you're my

favorite

[not]

hold this straight on your lap so the cheese doesn't get all over the lid i hate it when the cheese gets stuck to the lid. extra-cheese, the best part. they never put on enough pepperoni do they *please* chew with your ass wiped and *don't* make me smack you again. assholes off the table, please. you people have the manners of   peasants. close the lid. what, do you live in a *barn*?

[not]

i don't remember what time you were born — how the hell should *i* know — pardon my frankfries. it was a wednesday, i think, tho it was night and i don't remember whether it was before or after midnight. maybe you have far to go — who knows. for pity's sake give up on the woe haven't we had enough self-pity all crying is self-pity. you bake your bread you buy in it. there's no crying in this house. just

beds
we've made
you know
mattresses.

my sister and i shared the same four skirts and blouses on any given day we'd wear two of them so we had to do the warsh every other day on that scraping board in that cold water our fingers raw frozen blood. we ate squirrels and geese and sometimes rabbits. he could shoot a rifle but he couldn't cut the heads off the chickens i had to do it. i had to chase the

damn birds and get their necks on the board and — whomp. they were
dead. all i ever wanted in life was to buy meat at the butcher's you
remember that you with your books and this thing where you can't seem to
stop going to college. haven't you been in college long enough? i know
your kind: headed for bankruptcy. you probably qualify for food stamps by

yes, yes, you've told me, his family were butchers, you can tell from
your name

she cleans the breastbone and lets it dry so we can grab it one end each
and make a wish and
pull
and
snap!
it into pieces with our two pinkies. what's your wish?
you're not going to stop shaving your armpits, are you? like some of
those do. that's the last thing we need around here a hairy-pitted bra-
burner at the dinner table i'd like your politics better if you kept them in a
flatchest you and my sister.
christ.
one white supremacist and one women's libber. who will get the
breast meat?

[knot poet tree]

the papers dangle over the arm of the couch long yellow legal-pad paper with fine blue lines she doesn't quite stay between. the scrawl is huge and beautiful a script that leans heavily to the right and loops and curves and dances just like she did in the kitchen

transistor radio tinny.

aw, give it an 82, 'coz you couldn't hear the treble well enough to make out the lyrics but it had a beat.

sugar...aw, honey honey...you are my candy girl, and you got me scared to death songs of cravings, perfect for a kitchen dancefloor.

but here comes the news at the top of the hour never good because it came not from the mountains but from the city where people murdered trapped their kids in public school strikes.

three strikes and you're stupid.

i had a scholarship, you know.

he wouldn't let me go.

i had to turn it down and then i couldn't get another.

worked myself through state college lifeguarding.

it was the men who were the worst always diving head first into dark waters they knew nothing about snagging themselves on a tree root icy water attacking their hearts.

i dove and dove for dead

idiots.

i *always* write you the news of *my* life. long letters. i'm sending you my *journals* —

don't you understand? you know *everything* that's going on here. i
don't *complain*
like you. no, something's wrong with you you want something from me and
i can't guess what it is i'm tired of guessing it's time to end the riddle.

knock knock.

who's there?

nothing.

i understand. i understand that you just plain don't like me. what do
you want me to do?

nothing

she said

and hung up.

did you ever try to call her back?

i sent her a letter. she sent it back the hard way.

your wedding present, really, i called u.p.s. four times and they say it
was signed for how could you not have received it? are you sure you didn't
make a mistake?

i *told* you we were sending it.

you should take better care of your gifts.

i thought you would be happier

when you had a man.

[*nota bene*]

there weren't any fishes when we swam across well we didn't see any we didn't feel anything nipping our toes or anything like that like the minnows do when you wade in just up to your ankles. isn't it lovely to stand here and be in the sun look at the trees dark on the mountain. i'll get brown again this summer the register girl will scan the whole milk the wonderbread the fresca the poptarts the potroast the tampax

then ask me where i got that fantastic tan. in the caribbean?

i'll smile and say reading paperbacks in my backyard.

and she'll be impressed.

though it *has* occurred to me that she might be *more* impressed if i said it *was* the caribbean. if only i *could* go somewhere like you have the one who lives in the lucky generation women can do anything they want now be a biologist be childless be selfish be beautiful be in demand be rich forget where they come from, forget —

not poetry

what's that you said?

what did you mean?

hey, you two! get down here! get your heads out of your little dreams and get your butts down here! see? there's a cardinal! what do you mean where? i taught you to open your eyes underwater over there on the fence.

damn, we should paint that thing again this summer.

oh look the dog's chasing it out of the yard silly thing wouldn't know beauty if it handed him a gainesburger. beauty's all there is, you know? the science of beauty. what makes his feathers so red? how come his wife's feathers are so dull? how did all that happen?

well, ok, i can see you're as bad as the dog. it's all so stunning.

give me a kiss. love you. bedtime early tonight, right? you seem tired of me to late.

[that last part not useful, sorry, except to delay the inevitable]

did you ever try to call her, she asked, as we put one foot in front of the other in the steep air spitting a poxy sap crunching the squirrels whose heads were cut off at the neck toting seeds to their graves damn where did i put that fucking *acorn*?

[well]

well.

well.

it seems to me that if you're too frightened to dial a well-remembered

number

and risk the loss of love

then you are too frightened to love in the first place

and don't deserve the love god gave you.

you were *not* hatched under a rock you were once a pregnant thing.

(you were too.)

if you fear the loss of love you do not love.

love in blood blood in love death is the end of love but there are so

many ways to die.

here is one way:

"nothing,"

she said.

                                 not even poetry

and thus did she dis-in-her-it.

no poet in the trees

home to roost.

don't be obtuse. don't be so smart. oh, please. careful of the snake in
the ass. there aren't any fishes, and any way, i signed for it, put it in the
closet to save it for posthume and fucking forgot about it. fucking *sue* me. i
know how the lake sparkled, but the sticky stuff on the envelope, it got
stuck. i *know* i should have glued it, but there it is. dial me this, batman:
what's thicker than ashes, impossible to swim through? cruel and coerced.
as if *that* rhymes. they say it's all in the breast, you know — this diving for
the wed thing. since the mighty root was once an ovum like you. but the
most important thing, and you'd know this if you got your dead out of your
grass, is that a bathing suit can ride up on you and drive you beyond science

after poetry. so be careful with my sister's fictions. on tuscarora, they know

who stutters their sleds. which is important when the supply of oreos drops

below acceptable levels. don't cry: in the end

    your bed was made.

3:
Sentencing Phase

Part I: Where I'm From

Once upon a time, in a land far far away, a master-father castrated his daughter's long, apprentice sentences. Our tale begins in the master's dark, wood-paneled office, autumn leaves dashing against the ivy clinging to his window. He spends hours gripping red pen, pouring over the apprentice's promising young "stories." His eyes blur, his family calls (he *is*, of course, *married*)...but the daughter's "stories" would be saved. They would be trimmed, sculpted, sliced to order. She could be the new Ann Beattie, the clitorized Carver, if only he could make her so.

He toils and he sacrifices, gives the apprentice hours he could have applied to his own clipped, taut, Vintage(d) work. When she objects to the bloody scars on her manuscript he strokes his beard and sighs. If only she understood his sacrifice of time, of logos. Finally, in search of her father's agent, she relents. She slashes sentences, minimalizes pain, inserts projectile plot structures, offers in jest to add his name as coauthor. And ok, yes, she fucks him once or twice, since that is what the stroking of logos can lead to. Then she leaves his tutorial. And her sentences, like the vines near his window in spring, begin to grow back.

N.b.: These words are *not* chains binding you to any one specific construct of hardwood forests.

Part II: Where I'm From

Always clean up as you go.

"My mother is a poem I'll never be able to write/though everything I write is a poem to my mother."

Part III: Where I'm From

Memorize the turnpike tunnels: Blue, Kittatinny, Tuscarora, Allegheny. On South Mountain, Hosack Run spills down Methodist Hill, across Grave Ridge and into Conococheague Creek — north of Scotland, east of Iron Run, south of Dead Woman Hollow, west of Pine Grove Furnace. Fuller Lake is the cold one; Laurel Lake dams Mountain Creek; Cowan's Gap is better for swimming; Caledonia crowds in too many kids. Yellow Breeches Creek is best for trout and tubing, Conodoguinet for canoeing (the Seneca were better at it than we were).

One October day, a black swan lands on Laurel Lake, floats past the bright-red sugar maples, into the lily pads, around the bullfrogs — and vanishes into the low-branching pine forest behind it.

"I have arrived in Pennsylvania after an impossible trek."

Part IV: Where I'm From

She waits for him at Bigham's Fort. He's late — she fears the Delaware
have got him, imagines what they'll do to him if they have. She smiles at the
children, fails to convince them that there's nothing to worry about, rubs her
stomach where the new baby grows. Truth is, he's gone to Carlisle for salt, but
in the narrows near Bigham's Gap a bear has charged his horse and thrown
him. He's chasing his horse through the hills when the Delaware charge the
fort instead. He can smell the smoke for a mile before he sees it. She's sold to
the French, who bring her to Montreal. She breaks a leg running the gauntlet,
watches as they shove her sickly girl under the ice until she stops struggling,
watches as they let her float away. He will try, but never find her.

Her father drives nails into pine logs for a cabin while her mother burns out
the tree stumps. Shortly after her fifteenth birthday, she has just returned
from fetching the horse back from a neighbor, struggles with the harness, tugs
weakly, begs him to pull through the limestone rooted in the field that would
be corn. When the Seneca ride in bareback and snatch her from the plow,
she's wondering whether her brother left a little sugar with her biscuit lunch.
From the top of Piney Mountain, from her seat behind the man, she sees the
smoke of her father's pine logs twisting up between trees. When her release is
negotiated years later, she stays. Later, she will own her own farm, cut her
own cornrows, smother her own potatoes with her own dirt. Later still, she
will rent several farms to white tenants. She'll sleep on the floor with a
cherished husband, she'll bear sons who will kill each other, she'll become a

leader of her adopted people. To the white man who'll print thousands of copies but take out the part about her profitable orchards, she'll dictate the story of being captured by the people she loves.

Too near her stove, she stands rolling a pie. It's peach season. A. P. Hill and his men have walked a long way looking for shoes and supplies for the exhausted, but the mountain people have lost their tobacco farms and have nothing to give him. He's come down from Piney onto the flats. When he fires accidentally on Union Army scouts, Robert E. Lee has to get up, over, and down three mountains to defend Hill's position. From where she stands in her kitchen, she can't see them coming. She shoves sweat from her face with a floured hand. The heat melts the butter enough to make the dough sticky guns pop feverishly in the distance an occasional cannon shudders the floor carefully she lifts the edges of soft dough folds the circle in half folds the half-circle in half hefts the quarter-circle into the palm of her hand bullet tears through kitchen window into belly falls to floor hands high dough intact on her back soft circle of pie dough draped across   chest

The men searching for the three lost babes hike by her place on Wigwam Trail every morning for four days running. Occasionally they startle her by firing their rifles at a deer. They're nowhere near the right spot. She doesn't want to, but thinking of the children, she rides her mule over South Mountain and tells the sheriff where the children are. She's seen the place — in her sleep. The sheriff laughs her out of his office. Weeks later he has no choice but to check out by Kahler's place like she said. When the sheriff's men find the bodies of the children stacked trimly like firewood, he arrests her for murder.

How else could she

And why else would she tell, except to turn the guilt away from

Part V: Where I'm From

A 2-gravida female. Redhead. Current status unknown.

4:
Breeder's Digest

In the beginning — she said, relinquishing herself to our cultural need to establish endpoints and origins over and over — in the beginning, there was the awakening. She opens her eyes to a slit and turns her head to squint at the huge numbers on the digital clock. 7:33. She remembers *bereavement in their death to feel Whom We have never seen.* She rolls over, slowly, her back aching due to an insufficient mattress (someday we'll have the money to replace that thing), and reaches for the basal thermometer. She sticks the metal end under her tongue and lies back, still, sleepy, *Still nursing the unconquerable hope,* too groggy to purse her lips and hold the thermometer in place. She's not supposed to move around too much — that would increase her temperature — but she rolls over onto her side — closes her eyes — and with the thumb and index finger of her left hand — *So hopeless is the world without, The world within I doubly prize* — she squeezes her lips together.

Semen-idiotics. (*An honest tale speeds best, plainly told.*)

My husband — is an avid cereal box reader. (I live in terror of revealing his secrets but can't stop myself from writing.) We sit at the breakfast table in our small kitchen and he deconstructs the ingredient list *because I could not stop for* — what? Only 30 calories from fat, he asserts approvingly. One-hundred percent natural, he reads, and frowns. How does brown sugar count as natural? How? he insists? How? Exactly how do we define natural these days? (He needs something from me, some recognition that because he is being heard, he is alive.) Brown sugar is refined, isn't it? he says, and turns to stare right at me, demanding an answer. I roll my eyes and manage to like him anyway *because I could not stop for* — Tiny splashes of milk leap and stain the kitchen table as we slurp. One of us will wipe them up.

Because I could —

A girlfriend calls to ask how I am doing and I pick up the phone and listen while she tells me about the paper she has been writing for the last year. Something about music and how it's used as a metaphor in discussions of semiotics. I work to be A Good Listener, so I make affirmative noises — but also — *is there more? More than Love and Death? Then tell me its name!* — but also, I am in a bad mood of sorts and must struggle noticeably not to scream at her that I have *had it with semen-idiotics.*

He does the dishes. She makes the bed. She pinches him in the butt as he walks by on his way to the bathroom. He comes back. Will you look at this finger? he says. Does it look red and swollen to you?

On the phone, she asks me what I am reading, *Whither I went with a heavy heart, and down I sat with the picture of death in my lap.* I tell her nothing is safe, that I am caught in a synchronous web and the whole world is writing about what I don't want to think about anymore. For instance, I tell her, I read how the U.S. has one of the highest deaths-in-childbirth rates in the "western" world — one in 3000 — and how you're twice as likely to die of childbirth in the U.S. as in Canada — how you can walk over an invisible line and suddenly you are twice as safe — and I think we should all move north.

(I live in terror of revealing our secrets but cannot stop myself from writing, nor from sitting and staring as the toner on the page stares back at me, dead, the marker of some unknown grave.)

She is alone. She knows this not because she is really awake — or feels the loss of some presence — but because the bedroom door is shut. It is his habit to close the door so he doesn't wake her with bathroom noises when he gets up. Though his getting up itself is what usually gets her up. *Life is death we're lengthy at, death the hinge to life.* At which point she lies there in warm skin between warm sheets, looking at the closed door, sensing a day's light heating the east, a stick of glass beneath her tongue, her teeth clanging the glass, the stick resting perfectly between the gap in her two front teeth. The thermometer is difficult to read — *a tomb of rest and a cradle of hope* — so she twists the glass up and down in tiny movements until the toxic mercury flashes solid silver.

Hey. 98.2. Up from yesterday's 97.8.

Oh yes, and how you're nine times as likely to die in childbirth if you're forty than if you're twenty. Which is another kind of invisible line to trip over if you're not careful.

He is humming, imprecisely. It makes her laugh. She sneezes, he blesses her. She sings over him, trying to correct his key. He scowls playfully and tells her to knock it off. What should I do about my finger? he says. How are you feeling? he says.

On the phone, I listen — *Perhaps Death* — *gave me awe for friends* — and make affirming noises and manage not to scream at her that if women had been in charge of creating this language, there would be a special pronoun for mother-and-child. There would be a word for the weird subject position of a woman with a critter sucking her dark blood through roots dug down in the walls of her gut: *Love's unfathomable mystery.* "Part of me" does not cut it. "We" does not cut it. Is an apple not more than merely "part of" *The heart of human cruelty*, "part of" an apple tree? There would be a word for separate-but-same. Other but not. Any woman knows we need these words desperately.

Out of the eater comes forth meat, and sweetness out of the strong.

That gap in her teeth — the dentist calls it a diastema. The last time she saw her [ ], six years ago now — which then was the first time she had seen her in five years — her [ ] said, My god, look at that! You could drive a truck through there! She worries that resting the thermometer there every morning will drive the gap further apart.

98.2. Up from yesterday's 97.8.

Women from all classes and countries risked dying in childbirth or from infection afterwards. If the mother survived, frequently her baby did not. 1 in 4 did not live to be 5.

On the phone, she asks me what I am reading. *Without — the power to die* — I tell her that all of my books are overdue at the library. She pretends to scold me, but I tell her that life is a long series of overdue notices. Especially on *our* salaries, she says, and laughs.

He comes into the bedroom where I am reading synchronicity, *The idea of the Universe as organized around the act of perception.* Can I read this to you? he says. I put my book down and look up at him. Can I read this to you? he says again. He sits down next to me, looks tense, in-tense, mischievous, the skin baby-smooth and pinchable on his smiling face. I was looking up something about my finger, and I found this. In his hands, *The Merck Manual.* Hookworm Disease, he reads. Eggs are discharged in the stool — he reads — and hatch in the soil after a 1- to 2-day incubation period, releasing a free, living larva that molts a few days later and becomes infective to humans. The larvae penetrate human skin, reach the lung via the lymphatics and blood, ascend the respiratory tract, are swallowed, and, about a week after skin penetration, reach the intestine. They attach by their mouths to the mucosa of the upper small intestine and suck blood. About 25% of the world's population is infected with hookworms. Can you believe that? Twenty-five percent of the world's population.

In the course of my soliloquy I picked a flower at my side. It was pretty and newly opened, but an ugly caterpillar had hidden himself among the petals....

God, he says. We live on a completely different planet in this country.

(I live in terror of revealing...*the illusion of —*)

I just had to read that to you, he says.

What is interesting is that she found sense in the chance meeting of words.

It's possible I have arthritis in my finger, by the way. She takes his hand and kisses the pink lump on his swollen finger *more myself than I am.*

In the morning, after the bed is made, the kiss is long and dry and tender and (as they say in the novels) yearning. *Doomed defiant oneness.* They are not allowed to make love yet.

She has become obsessed with the fact that the seatbelt on the driver's seat of her husband's old car does not work. It would cost about a third of the car's total worth to have it fixed. When she drives it, she thinks she is going to die. When he drives it, she thinks he is going to die. She looks around the city — *For I have but the power to kill* — and sees at least 90 different ways that either one or both of them could die. She has become convinced that one of them will die and leave the other behind to suffer. There is nothing she can do to protect either of them. She starts the car and turns on the radio. *To be living in a moment you would die for — what more could you ask?* Charlotte Brontë died in her thirties (*A tear is an intellectual thing)* from complications in pregnancy, one year after she married.

In the old days every time a woman fucked she took death into her vagina.

In a dim room, on the monitor, a huge piece of black and white electronic pie, an *uncertain relation of opposition — Love and Death.* She can see the empty shades of gray hills rolling here, there. She can also see fragments. A piece of something here, a piece of something there. It puts her in mind of that plane crash in the ocean, the one that killed a mother she knew, and her child. The debris of a scattered sinking death.

When I am making the bed, he comes into the room, his morning smile broad on his face. I live for this smile sometimes. He puts his arms around me and pulls me in and his skin is — well — *the language of the heart has quite another grammar.* I run my fingertips up and down the curves of his hard, bare back and think of the hills and valleys of strong red sweetness he has given me. I close my eyes and think that I am holding him in the palm of my hand, with wonder, the way you would hold a scarlet hummingbird. Carefully, cooing at its wild beauty.

In the eye of the present, fragments of the past presents. She sees them remove a "specimen," a red-black piece of something several inches long — sees them put it in a plastic "specimen jar." She imagines it to be an arm or leg. A heart. She wonders what name they will put on the jar. *Nobody — I myself.*

98.2. Up four tenths *eternal in the human breast.* From yesterday.
In a gray world, from the other end of a tunnel — *twill be a Labor of surprise*
— there is the sharp, sorry stick of the dilators. Stay relaxed, they tell you.
It hurts less if you relax — (*semen-idiotics*) — so stay relaxed. Breathe.

The fleeing of absolute love beyond the borders of death into Myth

But. *Harp not on that strong, madam; that is past.* You should ice your
finger now, I say. I go to the freezer in the evening when he is not working
anymore and we are sitting on the couch watching the Bravo Channel —
Liberation from life — get four ice cubes, arrange them in a row on a frayed,
faded washcloth, close it around his finger. Should I go to a doctor? he says.
It's up to you, I say.

In the end — she said, because who can stop the end from coming *in the
deep bosom of the ocean buried* — in the end I live in terror of the words
defining the red, staring back at me mortal. And that is all.

5:
Composition as Explanation
of 137 Crop Circles

Having failed at one kind of production, regroup.

Get it right this time.

Decide you will live the dedicated life. Take a vow to poetry.
Establish that language controls. For years, ponder whether it's possible to
rebuild the master's house using the master's tools.

(Find the cost of freedom.)

Don't. Become a teacher who teaches that language controls.
Read nothing but Anzaldúa and Federman. Agree that white feminists
have long ignored the concerns of women of color. Bourgeois bitches like
you. Decide the next big thing will be the metrosexual minimalist, exiled
in Paris. Befriend and partner yourself solely to poets because "poets

don't finish their sentences" — after all, the sentence is finished, *nein*?

Remain an adjunct, eight (OK, nine) years out from your Ph.D. Ignore

raised eyebrows from your family..."Twenty thousand a year, no health

insurance, with a Ph.D.?" At Christmas dinner, argue that a Ph.D. is not

personally or socially worthless, even if it is valueless. Read Steinem's

"Revaluating Economics" 400 times. Worry about underemployment, since

there is no such thing as time. (Or error. There is only change.) Examine

the dedicated life, the empty 401(k).

Beat:

In literature, there must be conflict.

Said her department chair.

Don't be silly, she replied. I am not a hybrid writer. I'm a hybrid

thinker. After all, scientists have begun to suspect that 137 may once have

been 136. So Planck, you know, may not have been constant.

(Excuse me, but is this fiction?)

My best friend is Latina, said the white woman, butting heads at lunch.

I thought I was your best friend, said the Native woman, fork pitched into

mesclun greens — but you'll understand when you have your own children.

If all literature needs conflict, then all sentences require verbs.

Said her department chair, while sitting down.

(Where would this fall in Maslow's hierarchy?)

But wait, my other best friend is Canadian. I would not, after all (all

what, again?), want to debase a story with fact — but that *is* my final answer.

Huh. I figured you for an end person.

The wedding book, said the bourgeois bitch, recently divorced, butting heads at lunch, calls for a reception room with 12 to 14 square feet per person.

So the natural habitat of the wedding guest is 13 square feet??

Oh yes, and two bartenders per 100 people.

And don't forget to factor in fitting charges for your gown — not to mention a beading charge.

I see. Yes — one would not want beads falling bouncing crackling spilling all over the aisle people giggling pointing at the beautiful bourgeois butthead (recently divorced) bride on her Special Day because she was so cheap, the bitch, that she tried to glue-gun the beads onto the gown —

What was that about verbs?

OK, so my best friend is Latina, Native, and Canadian. First person, second person, and third person. But although we have I/we and she/they, we have no discernibly plural second person in English. Only you-you-you-you

(To her, this is a serious limitation.)

In the class taught by the persistently adjunct, the lovely young white woman (she majors in dance) displaying excessive skin reaches her arms up to braid her excessive hair and says, But we have to look at what's *happening* — we have to differentiate between writing that *represents* fragmentation, and actual fragment *in* the writing. Don't we?

In class, the lovely young Black woman (she majors in ethnic studies) fingers her dreadlocks with one hand and picks up her pen with the other and says, I just don't have any patience for poets who go off in the universe as if the reader isn't even there — how will anything ever change? In particular, a Native author needs to make even more sense than whites. Doesn't he?

(He?)

You accuse me of poetry, but surely you (of all people) perceive my obsession with the sentenced. Surely. Not to mention my refusal to middle.

In class, take nots [sic] on your current work in progress.

Excuse me, but I need to know, is I a word, or an image?

Asked the thesis committee chair, while seated. (Cf. "Ain't I A Woman?")

A good question indeed, and I do not know the answer, but it's not your story to tell, youse guys.

Here's the thing — the change *time-which-is-not-time* makes is often unpleasant. For instance:

Joe's Uncle Sam is having his leg amputated.

Excuse me, but this is not your story to tell.

Kass's father Norm has torn his rotator cuff.

Excuse me, but this is not your story to tell.

The difference between history and fiction, said the dean, is that they have distinct grammars, which must be respected in their distinctions.

Excuse me, but this is not your story to tell.

Wefour bestfriends embrace crop circles and are profoundly suspicious of theories of everything, especially those summed up by the number 137.

In the class taught by (see above), the honors student fingers her notebook and airs her voice, her favorite sound. I have no responsibility to Indians, she says — I mean, they've been selling themselves for years — they take gambling money from poor whites and use it to get drunk — that's their choice to do that — I'm not responsible for their lousy choices —

You know, said the department chair, standing up, it would be *very* OK if every piece of pose [*sic*] you ever fucking wrote was *not* autobiographical for fuck's sake. Given tenure and all.

Well, yes, but it nonetheless remains true that Uncle Sam cheats at rummy. This is OK, though, since this thing we call relentless time really is an endless revision. Sam says, Score's 4-2, and I say, Dammit, Sam, I'm four games up on you, cut the bullshit. Ten minutes before that I'd been up *two* games on the old coot lying cheating bastard for chrissake but I *lie* about that — that'll teach him, and I'm a teacher, and this is a teaching moment by fucking god because *I say it is.* So in this thing we call ten minutes, I go up one more game, he tries to take me down two, I make it up at three (that'll teach him). Then five weeks later I write about it and make up the whole thing about how I was cheating as well just to teach the old one-legged bastard a damn lesson.

I mean, I respect my elders. *Their* distinct grammars.

Meanwhile, there is the pain in people that this thing we call time forgot. In the class (etc.), she looks out over this new batch of victims, a new year, a new fall, a new chance to be someone completely new, someone completely of our own devising *This year I will be charming and lovable and roll with the punches and punishment and keep my sense of humor at all times* — and she can see it. The perfect spheres of damage, the scarred ovals of overly trimmed ego — and no tracks. No clues as to how the damage was done, no traces of who did it, a miracle of mowed-down human matters.

Excuse me, but this is not your story to tell.

And another thing, says the Latino student: there is a world of difference between what the writer intends and what the reader perceives. (And that's i before [ye], word and image, i i i i i.) And the biggest question of our time is whether it is *most* necessary (having established a hierarchy of reads) to memorize Mullen or Mullen or Swensen or Mayer or Hejinian.

Hashed over Hejinian. That would be a great title for some critical essay.

Yeah, great, some teeth-gnashing girl-bashing critical essay.

Said the teacher.

Go ahead. You can have the title. I thought of it, I said it, but you can have it.

And what you need to know is that Sam brightens right up when he hears me on the phone. (Norm never calls. And he still has legs. And grammar.)

Huh. Sounds to me (who?) like — it's long been — I mean, we are way overdue — Time for an *.

*

It's important to understand the rules before you can break them, said the creative writing program director.

But what about Rule 240? Most people don't know this, but if your plane is delayed, you can walk up to any airline personnel and say Rule 240 me, and they have no choice but to put you on the next available plane, with any airline, at their own expense should there be a cost differential.

And yet it would be ungrammatical to say so.

Then too, if while planning your wedding you use credit cards to make deposits on gowns and tuxedos, you create a paper trail making it easier to employ Federal Regulation C, which guarantees — regardless of any contract you signed forfeiting your deposit — a full refund of said deposit should your gown or tuxedo provider fail to deliver satisfactory goods.

On the other hand, if, like her, you believe heterosexual marriage (can't speak for metrosexual minimalists) is a fucking nightmare *This year I will be charming and lovable and roll with the punches and punishment and keep my sense of humor at all times* then perhaps you want to get out the glue gun, swear *semper fi* with a hand on your mutual photo album, kiss time goodbye, and right off the bat *allege the fitting charges* —

Or, you could simply start doing the Vowel-less Crossword Puzzle every Sunday morning, using this to mark what we used to call time but now call *change*, no no, *revision* — as in, y mrry m, I rvs y —

um, is Y a vowel?

and again, I am not clear, ain't I a word or image?

— which is to say, in "time" (obs.), you will measure your mutual revision thusly: Yes, that was back in volumeyear two of the album; or, No, you are quite wrong, that was the day we did puzzle five in volumeyear one — we were still newlypuzzleds then —

Hr hr — Y'll hv to fx ths — t's ll wrds nd n vwls, emailed the department administrative assistant, in the context of administering to the needs of —

Repeat after me (who?): I FIGHT BUREAUCRACY/ BUREAUCRACY'S ALWAYS WINNIN'

Since, you know, women make no sense, or so they say, so they fear for the timepieces we call lesbians — as for men, well, you just cain't — *Excuse me, but this is not your story to tell* and even if it were *This year I will be charming and lovable and roll with the punches and punishment and keep my sense of humor at all times* [obs.] but still *It's important to understand the rules before you can break them* DESPITE the fact that I FIGHT BUREAUCRAZY/BUREAUCRAZY'S ALWAYS

(Seems to me this would be an *excellent* time for a *second* * break, so that the first-person author may set upon a chair with the plural second person the more easily to eat her curds and NO WAY

*

And we're back after that word from our monster. Rereading the above, and absent any real revision, over time, anyway, what I'm thinking is that, as always, rejection letters will abound. Hemingway papered his shack with his, but, you know, that just wouldn't be me.

Huh. I'd figured you for all these years to be an end person — but the true danger, and I have said this before, will say it again, lies in the

damage over time, with no traces of cause. No past or future tension.
No explanation. Despite years of research, it happened time and time
again.

For instance, Norm's mother died when he was 16, and during the
war he was Heap Big Basketball Star but could not date because gasoline
was rationed — but this does not explain it (what?), does it?

My three best friends — yuns — are friends because they too live
the dedicated examined life. Over time [*sic*] we are able to help one
another rededicate. These four persons are all refugees from the bright-
sided sugar-sapped lemons-aided food-networked if-you-want-it-bad-
enough-it-will-happen NORTH AMERICAN BUREAUDRAWERS *would
you puh-LEASE put commas between your adjectives and would it to be
too much trouble to CLOSE YOUR PARENTHESES* Though all four drive
(relatively) recently-manufactured cars (but wait, she errs, one of us
does not know how to drive, an entirely pre-Steinemite urban
throwback), all four dispute the fondly held western notion that
grammar is designed to help people communicate effectively. Only one
had a wedding gown (as it happens, the same one that does not drive).
One understands the necessity for sewing rather than gluing beads onto
garments, and two speak a little German (one a lot) while two speak a
little Spanish (one a lot) and time [sick] will convince them that *only
women bleed*.

One has two children.

Which will have to do for all four persons, or so recent medical reports suggest.

One spoke her mind in her own home, resulting in the neighbors calling the cops with a domestic violence alert.

One paints, two write, one demonstrates.

One is made up.

Entirely fictional.

A bourgeois buttheading bitch of a non-bride, she would *never* be a bride, utterly invented.

Huh. Which bitch is false????

Time, or is it change, will revise them, just as 137 used to be 136. Which is to say, wefour was quite sure that the foundational universe-building sum of 1) Planck's constant; 2) charge of an electron; and 3) speed of light in a vacuum *what, you have a problem with semi colons now???*

could not possibly be a

prime

number

it *had* to have been revised over time [sick] from a multiple

And the fact that we're now *breaking lines* tells me it's Millertime {oy} for an ⋆ altho two of us must vacuum before cooking

⋆

I saw this goddamn novelpoem of yours — or is it poememoir — make up your mind — I know how you plan to drop gratuitous Spanish into your fiction like you're a Texas pol's speechwriter as if you didn't really get a pal

to help you cheat on your Ph.D. translation exams revising your translations

for you (what did you cook to bribe her? *arroz con pollo*? your best friend's

recipe, bitch?) your translations of the short fiction of Elena Garro — *your*

number is up, we got the goods on you, you're an imposter, not a real translator

of Mexican fiction your pollo *sucks even you're so white you insist upon extra*

seasoning just let the flavor of the schmaltz *for godsake sweat through the*

onions you were jewish once on your father's side 200 years ago back when you

were an indian killer back in the beginning of t___ before you were revised

excuse me, but AREN'T YOU TAKING THIS A BIT TOO FAR??

WHERE IS THIS VOICE COMING FROM??

christ. so punishing.

I've seen your goddamn novelpoem and your altitudinous pile of

rejections and there is no grammar here, since really, *it is the tenses in*

Spanish that will all but kill you

Norm bought you that expensive huge fat 20-pound door-stop

translation dictionary for the cerebration of your 33rd year (puzzleyear) on

this planet — this being mostly all he could grasp of what a Ph.D. does/is

for (you after all attempting to revise yourself via the intensive study of

Chaucer, Sterne, and students

translation is impossible. so punishing.

the verbs

you getting after all so infertile so late in your t___/revision/puzzleyear

a phd (for what, again?) slowing down your tenureclock

"We refer you to the table of irregular verbs."

"The Subjunctive is widely used in Spanish, mainly in subordinate clauses dependent on expressions of possibility or probability and conjunctions introducing future, hypothetical or contrary ideas or actions; in general, all statements involving conjecture or guesswork, and all statements expressing not knowing or believing, negation or doubt

as in

dude que lleguemos a tiempo

HEY! SEE THAT?? SHE'S DOING IT ALREADY!! I TOLD YOU SHE WOULD!!

in which by *a tiempo* we really mean *by the next puzzleyear*

which is to say, translate "revision" to mean "change" to mean "tiempo"

and now a moment for another word from our

*

Pardon me, said our college president — the same one who voted no on same-sex domestic-partner YOU AND YOUR HYPHENS!! (not to mention adjunct) health insurance — Pardon me, she said, but do you plan to footnote those quotes there?

Assimilator.

[So. This being the fifth section of this proem pose (?), and what with her being up 4 points *rummy!* and having 3 friends 2 of whom speak Spanish and 1 of whom used to be jewish, whatsay we wrap this fucker?]

TO REVIEW: Decide (she did). Dedicate (she did). Read only memory
(she did). Rebuild grammar (she tries). Make change. Revise (again and).
Use [insert punctuation mark here]. Cross words in puzzlement. Consult
model verb charts (paradigms) over revision. For instance:

Pretérito imperfecto subjuntivo (s-form)

siguiese	siguiésemos
siguieses	siguieseis
siguiese	siguiesen

Then, abolid los verbos.

{Follow me?}

Because you can.

And all this because there must even if there is no time at all in the
composition there must be time in the composition which is in its quality
of distribution and equiliberation [*emphasis mine*].

Students finger braids. Cannot stop talking even though there is snow
in the high country *already this year* and Black Swan drifts south for winter.
No glue gun would bead their time in such a way as to make it matter to the
causeless human pain *not your story* and by the way, this be *fake prose*?

Well. You *told* me to make lemonade on the bright side for all time to
revise. At least for my next trip to Paris.

Didn't you?

I mean, hybridity aside, I got my commas *pretty* straight, controlling my
quotes *mostly* and parenthetically closing *most of the time* for 136 whole

thoughts now. Planck being constant and all.

Right?

And this even though, having taken you for an end person, there was in the beginning the time in the composition there was in the beginning confusion a continuous present but in literature in sentences in verbs there must be time.

And afterwards, that is all, Max.

Regroup.

Get right with change.

6:
Accidental Species

*Accidental species are rare birds that do notbreed regularly
or occur annually in North America, but whose presence
has been accepted by the American Ornithologist's Union.*

— *National Audubon Society Field Guide
to North American Birds: Western Region,* 1994

Tableau vivant: She sits — this was before chapter 1 — she sits at
lunchtime at her kitchen table with a man she thinks she knows fairly well,
since he works at the college where her soon-to-be-ex-(yes, there was
another)-husband used to work, having just cheated on her soon-to-be-ex-
husband with this man who is also cheating on his wife, who is pregnant, by
the way — eight months pregnant — sitting at her kitchen table with this

man whose first act, upon entering this marital aerie, was to bend down and pull a tiny .22 pistol out of his sock — thereby making it easier to get his worn jeans off — sitting there with this man who then placed that small, shiny gun on the kitchen table next to the white paper napkins in the red plastic napkin holder — she and this man sit eating hot dogs they have boiled on the stove in a small Revereware pot with stained copper bottoms (she should polish those...);

and the *cleaning* lady, someone she has hired to help her with her busy life despite the profound feelings of good, Pennsylvania German, post-Mennonite, working-class guilt this causes — after all, shouldn't she sweep up her own shit? — the cleaning lady walks through the unlocked back door, the kitchen door she unlocks every Thursday morning before going to work at her office at the theater —

the *cleaning* lady walks through the unlocked back door about a half an hour early and stands and looks at the two of them, *her* hand frozen on the doorknob, *their* jaws frozen in mid-wiener-munch — the *cleaning* lady's mouth gapes while theirs jam shut;

and as they all freeze there, staring at each other, their minds flying over what this looks like and in fact most obviously *is* — and as they all freeze there, staring at each other in something a little bit like horror, *the phone rings* —

the phone *actually rings* —

and with a shared psychic certainty that can only occur when one person has caught two other persons with their pants down (so to speak), all three know without a doubt that the caller is her soon-to[etc.], phoning from his new office at his new job in a new college nine hundred miles west of there.

All three swallow.

First, be 14. Sit on your neighbor's porch and feel the intensity of
shyness, of isolation, of *please don't look at me, please look at me, please don't*
look at me, please look... and see a distant look in the eyes of the Puerto Rican
boy you have a crush on, and know you'll never flirt with him for real, for
serious, because at 14 you already know that your [ ] would not appreciate
your bringing him home, that she would be nice, polite, but that the slightest
shocked look would cross her face for a millisecond — because you know
complexion is thicker than love — but anyway, sit on your neighbor's porch
and watch that distant look of his, feel your aloneness, think about it, and
decide suddenly that he is feeling exactly what you are — thanks to which,
you now know he is afraid *you* don't like *him* — *look at me don't look at me*
look — and know he fears he is not attractive, charming, likeable, loveable,
and that he wants to belong — to whom? — to borderline whitetrash kids like
you up the street? — and that he doesn't want his parents meeting you either,
that his parents would not even bother being polite *los costarían demasiado* —
     so go home and decide that
     if you put yourself in his shoes, you can see what he's feeling, and that
     you can become him.
     Can't you?
     Second, don't forget to alienate your family. Become the soothsayer, the
person at the Thanksgiving table who insists we acknowledge the National
Indigenists' Day of Mourning, said insistence occurring while passing russet
potatoes mashed so aggressively that they've become elastic — and while
you're at it, hiss at every racist joke, race your heart over every sexist jibe, tell

them everything they refuse to accept about who they really are, who you are (really) — and while you're at *that*, be sure, when you crawl the bars looking to get laid — this was (just) before herpes and well before chapter 1 — to choose partners who are outspoken radicals, preferably from the working class —

and bring them home, set them loose on your family *please curb your dog* — insisting that you are a race traitor a gyn-ecologist a vegetarian — so that soon they stop visiting you, and, for purposes of self-preservation, stop reading your writing — not even when you make it easy for them — not even the crumpled photocopies of your publications in obscure journals, delivered by the postal carrier during the hour they typically spend in the local pub — so of course *forget* expecting them to cross the street to the bookstore to pick up the literary tabloid for which you write witty reviews of great merit that revise the very *notion* of *review*, and TOTALLY forget them clicking on the web site of the groovy online journal for which you compose clever cultural critique. By all means, *do* decide you descend from alcoholics, and mourn the premature death of your living family.

Not to mention your ovaries *the buck stops here.*

Finally, rewrite their stories over and over again.

What do you mean you don't believe it? She sits with spaghetti tangled around her spoon. She gapes at the man across the table and reaches forward to sip some wine. Her stomach hurts. What do you mean it lacks credibility? What is there not to believe? You think I would make this up?

It just sounds like an unlikely story, he says.

An unlikely story, huh?

OK.

Let's try this again. It's 1982, the Equal Rights Amendment is dying a slow death attended by candlelight vigils, I'm out of work, I'm so broke I'm going to bed hungry at night after only one meal a day, bought and paid for by my boyfriend — a man, by the way, who will later stalk and beat me — and I decide, hey, I have nothing to do, I might as well work for women's rights, and I juggle my job interviews with my vigil-holding, and I'm five-foot-ten, so what keeps happening is that they keep tapping me to go stand in the middle with the signs because I'm tall enough to obscure the signs being held by the pro-life counter-demonstrators, and then the Abortion Control Act is introduced as legislation, Pennsylvania the first state to introduce a bill designed to curb Roe v. Wade, and now I'm on the capitol steps in Harrisburg with my signs, and one night I'm on TV and the next day I have a job interview and the guy says to me, "I saw you on TV last night," and the interview lasts five whole minutes, because it's a P.R. job, for chrissake, and the last thing you need controlling your media exposure is a liberated hell-raiser — what *was* I thinking — so that interview is a total waste of gasoline I don't have and I cry the whole way home, and the ERA dies of a disease called patriarchy, and now we've got this Abortion Control Act which would have been stopped if we had an ERA in the first place, and I'm busting my ass, getting postcards signed to legislators and using what's left of my gasoline to drive to the state house, and the TV cameras are rolling and I'm in the rotunda, under that huge dome, in the midst of all that marble and all that sober power to do good, and I'm up on the top step — and this man, he's maybe 55 or so, and maybe a little taller than me, he's got this huge poster on a stick, just like mine, and mine says "KEEP GOVERNMENT OUT OF THE BEDROOM" and his doesn't say anything, it's just a huge picture of a thumb-sucking fetus in a womb, the uterine sac collapsed, the blood gushing out of the placenta being sucked from the wall, and the woman in charge of the rally yells at me to cover his sign with my sign, which is what he's been doing to me, and I move my sign out from behind his and put it in front of his, and he does the same, and every time we do this dance we have to lean a little bit more forward on the capitol steps, narrow, only about three inches high, marble, and he's wearing this white dress shirt, and a blue tie, and a red sweater over the tie, and a blazer over that, and dress slacks, and shiny shoes, which shoes I get to study well while I look down to map out my struggle for space on the narrow steps, and I'm thinking, What is this nice man doing pushing me around like this? because his sweater is itching my arm, he keeps pushing against me, and I'm frightened, and I can feel his fury, and when I meet his eyes, he despises me, and I've done nothing to him, I haven't even *had* an abortion, not that there's anything wrong with that, but I'm predisposed to miscarriages — which, by the way, my doctor calls spontaneous abortion — and I'm baffled by the moral difference there — but anyway, I decide to end the struggle and I move away, give up, move my sign to the side so that both can be seen — but he won't *accept* this, and *follows* me, *chases* me, *works* to cover my sign with his and now it's all I can do stay on the steps, I'm clinging to the edge of marble like a sparrow clings to wire, because he's pushing me and glaring at me, and I have never felt someone *hate* me so much — well, except maybe my [ ] — and I keep moving to the side to make room for myself, leaning forward — while down below the woman in charge of the rally is flapping her arms up by way of saying that I should get the sign *higher*, and OK, now I'm up on *tip-toe*, and then I hear, "DIE, EVE'S CHILD" —

    — and the next thing I know I'm tumbling down the marble stairs crashing into a hundred people whose bodies don't stop me but only bounce me toward the marble railing where finally I crack my head

and lie in a heap at the foot of the rally

the speaker looking down on me from her position at the podium.

And I stand up, and I brush myself off, and I clutch my stomach, grab hold of this womb this man thinks he owns, and scream back at the man, who stands looking down on me with not one expression on his face, not one. And I scream, "YOU FUCKING BASTARD, YOU SAY YOU GIVE A SHIT ABOUT *LIFE* WHEN YOU PUSH SOMEONE DOWN THE STEPS LIKE THAT!" And the capitol police who have been a few steps away the whole time lean down and pick me up. One cop on each arm. And I came to this capitol to visit as a child, with school trips, with my father, who brought me here and taught me to respect the political system. Of the people by the people and for the people will not perish but have everlasting life. And one cop looks at me with complete irritation and does not mean it when he says, "You all right, miss?" And the other cop looks at the first one and says, "She don't want to be pressin' no charges, I'm bettin'" — which pair of dangling gerunds reminds me once again that I live far too close to the fucking Mason-Dixon Line. And they let go of me and look at me, and I'm just the biggest pain in the ass of their lives. And the speaker's looking down at me with shock on her face and the TV cameras are rolling. And I realize that the one from Channel 8 is two feet from my head, which I touch, which is when I discover that blood is running down my neck. "Fuck you people!" I yell at the cops. And push outside, away from the rally, away from the domed rage and the lethal marble and the evil man who would prefer to see me dead than speaking my mind about my own fucking stomach. And I should've gone to the hospital for stitches but I didn't. And I went home and saw myself on three different channels, film at 11, though Channel 8 had the best angle of the blood on my dress. And I had no job interviews so I stayed in my apartment for three straight days and didn't answer the phone and didn't go out to see my boyfriend or to eat his food. And I never went to another rally again. Not for nuclear power, not for women's rights, not for the environment, not for unions for president for anything. It's been seven years, and here I sit. Doing nothing.

Now, what about that story don't you believe? she asked, her heart pounding. The wine glass shook in her hand.

He stared at her blankly. I just don't believe it, he said. It's too outlandish.

You don't believe there are men like him, or what? What part don't you believe?

I'm sure there are men like him. But they don't act out that sort of anger. The system doesn't permit it.

Really. I see. And yet every word of that story is true.   Well. Just about.

See? he said. I told you. Which part isn't true?

I didn't shout the thing about life at him. I didn't say anything. I was stunned stupid. Stunned silent. And the part about the cops. They stood on the other side of the room. They kept their arms crossed the whole time. They never made a move. They just stared at me. So I left. And another thing I thought was weird was that not one woman from N.O.W. ever called to see if I was OK. I never saw them again, and they never missed me.

There. You see? So it's not true.

But it's mostly true! And if anything I made the cops look *better* in the story. The assholes.

I'm sorry, I just don't find it credible. You should be writing about a more significant subject matter.

She threw her fork onto her plate and ungently set down her wine glass.
She bobbed her head forward and pushed through her long curls with her
fingers. Feel this! she shouted. Feel this! I have the scar! She reached
forward for his hand, tried to grab his fingers, to guide them to the truth.

He leaned back in his chair, looked around at nearby restaurant
patrons, and shook his head. Why do you get so emotional? he said.

Which is when she sees that he's gazing at her with the same non-
expression fetus-man had beamed at her that day on the capitol steps.

She whips the napkin from her lap, throws it across the table into his
face, grabs her purse, stands up, walks briskly across the restaurant, and
hails herself a cab.

Or that's how she tells it these days. Actually, she gazed back at him in
dismay, pushed the pasta around her plate with her spoon, passed on
dessert, changed the subject matter to something that didn't matter, like his
career, and fucked him three or four more times before deciding that she
really needed to find a new creative writing teacher.

You're writing about me, I can tell, he (his brother) says. They're sitting
in front of the television, a Broncos game on. He's got a bet going with
Uncle Dominick, ten bucks if the Broncos break this unbearable losing
streak that has the entire city utterly demoralized. Ah, for the good old days
when John Elway wasn't just a guy who sold Chevies off I-25. You're writing
about me. I know you are. You ask me all these questions about the fucking
t-nut he has to buy to fix the table leg and you listen and listen and listen
and I can just tell you're going to leap up during halftime and go take notes.

Just then (saved by the ACL) the running back destroys his ACL on a
play. Whatever that is — something in his knee — but the whole city will
talk about it for days. ACL. Anti-Christ League? Abject Courtly Love?

Association of Cunt Lickers? Whatever. The local news will lead with the
ACL-in-the-knee story, right in the middle of a series of serial murders of
homeless men on the other side of town from the football stadium. And
he'll scream at the television set. Christallfuckingmighty! he'll yell. NOW
what the fuck are they going to do?? With no fucking RUNNING BACK??
They got no QUARTERBACK, now they got no RUNNING BACK?? Now
my fucking UNCLE is TEN BUCKS RICHER. He (his brother) grabs the
remote and snaps off the set.

You're going to go write about this, aren't you? I know you're writing
about me. I can tell.

It was lousy sex anyway, all about his small teacher's penis and big
teacher's belly and scratchy teacher's beard. Here's something that really
happened: the first time they slept together, at her house (in the guest
room), he came inside her after, oh, I don't know, 45 seconds — not that
that has anything to do with her orgasm anyway — then crawled off her, got
out of bed, dropped to a chair across the room from where she lay seeping,
and said to her, "This is where I'm not a very good lover."

(*This* is where?)

(*This??*)

So what did she do?

She smiled reassuringly, and returned to her role as ho-stess (stress on
ho). "Can I get you a towel?" she said. (She actually said.) He nodded. She
got out of bed and took one from the linen closet across the hall, 10 cc's of
ruin running down her thigh.

So, as you can see, it helps a lot if you dump that teacher you're sleeping
with and go for a Ph.D., which is more than he has, by the way, not that this

is a competition, and take exams with a bunch of scholars who will ask you to read Julia Penelope and tell you that language is a failed tool, that communication is a myth, doesn't really happen, that language was invented by men for men, that it doesn't work for women, that the construction "Sarah was raped" utilizes a passive verb that provides, as we'll discuss repeatedly, for no agency, no responsible party — which is to say, WHO THE FUCK RAPED SARAH??, and that even our masculinist nominatives fail to describe, as we'll discuss repeatedly, the relationship between a fetus and its host, a fetus and its sire — that, to name an oft-cited example, the word hysterectomy was created by men to describe a lunatic experience, that luna is feminine and comes from moon, which is to say loony tunes, that moon is related to mood and mood is related to mod and mod is related to modicum and that when it comes right down to it women have but a modicum of power over their hysterectomies — not to mention ovaries — not least because the rhetoric is stacked against them.

Fuckin'-A *right* it is.

But you have *free will*, says my eager male student in my women's literature class, the one guy who's *not* there to cruise chicks during small-group discussions. He's a philosophy major, and at the age of 19 has already been botched by Locke. You have the choice of *redefining* yourself in some non-masculinist way, he says. And aren't these all vast generalizations, anyway? Aren't we stereotyping women when we complain that they have no control over language?

Oh, shut up. Just shut up. Here's your fuckin'-A. Go away.

"You're going to write about me," her [ ] said. "Of course you'll write about where you come from. A writer writes what he knows."

"Well," she replied indignantly, "thank you so much for the fucking *male pronoun*, M__, but setting that aside for the nonce, as indeed I am frequently forced to do as a woman writer, again let me say that you should lay your fears to rest, because this is also the age of *mobility*, of the transferable *worker*, the portably *potted*, the ceaselessly *plotted*, a situation that's even worse in Hack-a-Dame, which is of course where I will earn my paltry living because it permits me at least *some* time to write, and boasts at least a *few* people who share at least *some* of my bookish qualities, and also by the way I'm a half-way decent teacher because I Teach The Conflicts, even though I hate conflict, as you know better than anyone since I have never had the ovaries to fight you, you, my Conflict Of Origin, my C.O.O. — and by god if the COOZ shits, WEAR her — so no worries, darling, I'll be moving between four different time zones for very likely more than a decade, and then I'll be so accustomed to moving and to living without real community that, despite my rather serious case of heim-vay, the German notion of land-sickness, a disease to which (essentialist) Germans are particularly susceptible, and despite my origins as a regionalist writer, an Appalachian writer, a northern Appalachia landscape writer, as if regional writers have a hope in hell in this postmobilist age, a writer who knows a bit about scrapple and pizza and cheese steak — Yo, Vinnie, if it ain't a good roll it ain't a good hoagie! — and, most important, a writer who *knows*, really, dearest, don't shit yourself, *very little about you and this place*, and who has moved around so much that all that's left is a persistent romanticization of Place de Ville — don't worry, dearest, I'll end up hiking some much craggier scarier jaggier peak on the Front Range and harkening back to the good old days of Appalachian walking, where no one needs a walking stick and pepper spray, and everyone has bad knees because there are no passes through the hills of Appalachia — I mean, come on. Relax."

And so. You must prepare yourself.

The following contains an objective correlative about truth, and I don't give a good shit if you don't believe it:

In a bar in Fort Lauderdale there's a pink flamingo, live, wings clipped, chained in a pool of neon-lighted water, a fountain tossing colored drops behind him — a bar where, across the room, a man plays piano, waitresses buzz around in pink feather leotards and pink spiked heels, carrying trays full of umbrella drinks — and you and I sit at a table watching it all — watching the flamingo, who stretches his head high into the humid smoky air and lifts one foot —

— which is how I see he's chained — bolted to the room by thin shiny metal that clinks and splashes the water as he stands fidgeting —

and you tap your foot to the music and smile at our waitress who winks back at you like I'm not there while you scratch the new sunburn on your arm, the t-shirt we picked up at the beach stretching across your chest, and you take my hand and I watch you play with my fingers —

— and I hate you for not being upset by this.

You laugh and say What's the point? Don't get yourself crazy over something you can't change.

Something you can't change?

I hatch my plans. I ask to see the manager, lean over that huge bowl of pink mints by the cash register and say in some threatening voice I really do have but have never used — anyway, in my unused threatening voice I announce that I refuse to spend money in an establishment that would choke a beautiful bird with smoke and chains —

I'll wait for you in the car, I say, and get up and walk through the smoky maze of tables and pink waitresses and past the mints to the lit, Lauderdale night.

I slam the car door behind me. I close my eyes to the leather-smelling quiet. The manager wilts as I speak, my threatening voice collapsing his spine like an accordion — he stammers, his face contracts, his shoulders tense. Why yes, of course, he says. We'll remove the bird immediately. Please pardon the offense.

He picks up the phone and barks an order as I lean back.

Thank you, I say, and return to my seat, reach for your hand, play with your fingers, watch your eyes stretch wide with amazement as two sweet, frothy umbrella drinks are set before us, brought by a waitress in long bermuda shorts and thick-soled walking shoes — who smiles at me gratefully. Compliments of the house, she says, just as two men appear, lean into the water, unchain the bird and walk it through the bar, right out the front door.

The bird walks slowly, lifting one long, nimble leg after another, leaving webbed droplets of water where his feet fall on the tiled floor, his head high, looking at no one as he stops at the glass doors, waiting for the men to push them open.

I love him very much for the way he holds his head, for the way he makes no fuss, for the careful way he places his dripping feet.

The car door slams.

You settle heavily into your seat, the car shaking under you — you fit the key in the ignition and start the engine — and without looking at me, ask: What do you want to do now?

I look at the clock on the dash. You have kept me waiting a full fifteen minutes —

— and suddenly I wish I had something electric, a cattle prod maybe, something that would stun you a little, leave you a little confused, something for those times when you can't even see how wretched you're being —

I feel a little tired, I say. I'd like to get to bed.

On the way to the hotel you stop for a six-pack at a liquor store plastered with neon signs — *CERVESA FRIA* — and in the room you fill the bathroom sink with ice and plunge in the beer — *muy fria*, for chrissake — not thinking that maybe I might want to wash my face — so I just get in bed — ask you to turn the fucking TV down — I mean, really — roll over, cover my head with the blankets to black out the blue light of the box, listen to the hum of the air conditioner, the spurts of the laugh track, until I am no longer hearing

until I wake up sharp with a chill, the room gray, quiet but for your snoring — what woke me? — fear — don't know what of — my heart is loud in my head —

so I lie back, watch the shadows on the wall, listen to my heart, a steady thud, breathe deep, soothe it slow

but it beats on, without me, heedless, too strong, too weak

Then I remember the bird. And my heart grinds out a skip. I have done something awful, something unforgivable. I have betrayed the bird.

I left him there alone.

But no. I could write a letter, tell the management I'm never coming back with that bird chained in that gray smoke, tell the management I'm telling all my friends that they should never ever patronize a place that would so patronize birds.

It could work! I watch as the men duck their heads to lower the bird into a limo, watch the bird settle softly in the back seat, pink boa-feathers ruffling in the breeze of the open window, bumping down I-95 to Miami and then over to the swamps, over to the Everglades — see him step out, glide one foot forward into damp black earth, lift his beak to sniff the dark, humid air, smell the life-giving rot beneath heavy hanging trees, smell where he belongs.

In the distance his eye catches late sun reflected in a shallow pool, where he hears the call of his own, and begins to walk towards the lake, begins to run, to flap his broad wings and beat the thick air — not flying — run-flying — kicks feet and wings — trips through earth water air for dear life — and is — gone — mixed with a flock — which is he and which is they? — they are he — they are we — of tall, spindly pink birds run-flying in the distance, legs lunging past lolling, moss-drooping trees, across silver weed-water darkening in the glades, their pink feathers dimming and ready, dying sun to their shoulders,

while I stand waving, missing us all already.

There now. Did you get it? Do you see it?

I know you're writing about me, s/he says. I can tell.

You're so vain — you prob'ly think this proem's about you — don't you. Don't you.

You're so vain!

My [ ]'s male-pronoun writers — the fact that Jack raped Jill — the syntax for missing — these are the things that plague. That, and ova. Since, really, most of what goes on in life has nothing to do with how I reach orgasm (*can I get you a towel?*). Although I do not breed regularly, my presence has been accepted in North America. Except for when I tell the truth. You fuck me, I write you. That's the deal. If you lack the *cujones*, hit the road.

(She said, scooting down to the end of the table and fitting her feet into the socked stirrups *Stir it up — little darling, stir it up!* — bored, waiting for her second husband [some people never learn] to come back with the sperm — where the fuck is the sperm, honey?? — we don't have all day here!! — then wincing as the nurse bounds in, holds a small test tube up to her face — "Is this your sperm?" the nurse demands — and she looks at the nurse like she's from Mars, which causes the nurse to jiggle the test tube again, impatiently, as if to stir the contents *Stir it up!* — and she looks at the maybe quarter-inch of clear fluid in the bottom of the test tube — *is that all there is??* — and notes her name on a slip of paper taped to the top of the tube — *FLEISHER* — while the nurse barks, "We go to great lengths to be sure we have the right sperm, OK, so, *really*, I have to hear you say it, and I need to know: *Is this your sperm or not??*"

("It's my semen, and I'll cry if I want to," she says.

(The nurse frowns.

(Sperm, sperm — said the breeder with her feet in the stirrups — where the fuck is the sperm?? Has the man come with the sperm yet???)

Cleavage had never been a thing in her flatchested life, but here she was cleaving.

As if.

All three swallow.

(*Tableau mordant:*)

Simultaneously, both women speak:

"I'll start on the upstairs."

"I'd better answer the phone."

The cleaning lady vanishes with the Vanish.

The goodly guilty Pennsylvania German, post-Mennonite chick gets up from the kitchen table, reaches for the phone on its wall cradle, carries the receiver around the table and out of the room, pulling the cord.

"I thought you'd be there," he says. "I was just thinking about you, and I had a feeling you might come home for lunch. What're you eating?"

Her voice is thin: "Oh, that's sweet.... Um, I sort of have my hands full here...can I get back to you?"

"Call me tonight, then."

She stands there with the phone in her hand, with the line dead, the cord twisted, pulled far out away from him, for longer than she realizes.

Eight months pregnant, she thinks.

Deserve's got nothin' to do with it. (Clint Eastwood once said.)

(He'd get her back later, when they divorce, demanding rights to the stories she wrote during their marriage. About him, of course.)

The big-bellied, towel-dried man sits at the kitchen table, hunched over his plate, eating the last of his hotdog, using the last little bites to sweep up any onion, pickle and mustard that might have fallen free. Precisely, he licks each fingertip on his right hand. He takes a white paper napkin from the red plastic napkin holder next to the .22 pistol on the table and slowly, carefully, wipes every trace of relish from his beard.

7:
Genealogy

Ultimately, in the midst of going from OINK (one income no kids) to DINK (double income no kids), in the midst of diagramming the sentence that is her family tree, she will discover that she descends from no one. Her white blood splashed red blood, relating her to nothing. Prelating her only to the properties of family.

Which is to say, I went home to discover the predication of our denial. Which is to say, we are those who *did* that and since we *did* that we are *they*. We are *of* that property. Which is to say, those that splashed in order to own, they are we, and we are we due to that property. Fenced. Naturally.

(This would be Part One.)

Propertied: in which one is *of* what one *has*. Thus is the familiar properly tied. Plus, one must be born to be reborn (*i.e.,* follow the dinky-binky spider up the water spout). Norm is diagnosed with idiopathic familiar syndrome — something *we* get, but not genetic; rather, something peculiar to *us* arising from *no cause.* Thus has our propertied syndrome no agency — a sickness branching out from our familiar. We share with it the property of having no cause. It has none and neither have we. A cause.

No cause, no agency, simply a relation. He has it, he had it, you have it, it is not ideal, not near ideal. A simple sentence arranged upon a vast-stretching hemlock (you know, state tree of corn-rowed, double-dutched Pennsylvania). And if my English is not your English, then still it may be said that all of our Englishes have one thing in common: none of them contain synonyms. None of us may be the same. Logically, then, we may predicate that within our various species of the genus English, none of us contain the properties we call opposites.

His father died quietly, without speaking.

Her father, as noted, is the normanator. Familiarly, this makes her the *ab*norm — which is to say, the *from*norm, *not*norm being notpossible in our English. Ever logical, Triptolemus posited that it could happen: that the child may be the blood of the parent, but the parent is not necessarily the blood of the child — this possible because the child is begot by the parent, but the parent is *not* begot by the *child.*

No, no, think about it, it makes sense. If there is no sameness, no synonym, there is no difference. No opposite. I'm right about this. For instance: what is the opposite of power?

See? I'm right.

She inherits [*sic*] various idiopathic syndromes, the worst of which is an ideopathology: the sickness of an idea'd sentence. For Christmas, they gave her A Keeper: the imp gestures *SHH!* Thus do they hint at silence, diagramming their elimination of agency. *The imp gestures.* Theirs is time without end, verb without object, establishing property. Or, if you prefer, they establish an accidental prelation of difference.

I do my best to chart the familiar synonym, though I am no Mendel and breed no pead words — a tendency which results in epistasis. The idiopathic etymology of the sentence involves the suppression of one gene by a nonallelic gene — making of allele any of the alternative forms of verbless genes that can occur at a given locus — for example, one might have red cunt hair, say, or, brown cunt hair — these being one set of alternatives available — and my point here is that, aesthetically, at least, she suffers from an allelic tendency to skip verbs altogether — since, finally, options may be available, but choice is not —

— so then, absent a consult with Fra Mendel, should I conclude that my own linguistic epistasis is the suppression of one red cunt hair gene by another red cunt hair gene? — or does it mean simply a change in alternatives — for instance, offering as new possibilities either the green thumb or the red thumb —

— and I cannot speak for the rest of my family in this regard, but I suspect they are anti-cunt —

— and so, to return to the matter of your English versus my English, in what ways does your English shush my English — if the imp pens poison —

And given our treed family's failure to produce opposites, how could I *not* be obsessed with *our* sentence. Since we are ideopathically familiar in our syntax.

Your expressions, you see, descend from nowhere. Your sentence may be predicated on tradition, Triptolemus, but it is clear that tradition may not be predicated on the sentence. The sentence is the *child* of tradition and therefore need not be the *parent* of tradition. There *is* no grammatical allele — there is only the unborn rebirth of the *from*norm, for no attributable cause, diagrammed to oppose opposites in our Englishes — an accidental agency.

What else is to be done with a grammar which tolerates neither sameness nor opposition?

They insist upon their right to the familial ideopath — we are not them; rather we are we — but unpredictably, violating all five categories of logic, they will not permit the individual ideopath, the I am not we. They sigh over the *from*norm but will not choose the *not*norm

tempting us to avow that just because the sentence has traditions does not mean I have to *maintain* them — and here the imp is predicated upon us — since we maintain — we being the subject of an objectfree predicate — the object being you — from which we conclude that the genealogy of the sentence is all *about* predicates — about the existence of action — the action of existence — the existence of property — the action of property — *does* she act, *does* she exist, or *is* she *not*?? — *and how* — and yet we have yet to permit precise responsibility for the idiopathic cunt —
isn't action actually about time?

but there is no time, there is only change
we read

where was she?

the progeny of verbs — since desperately she tries, she is back there trying, don't you hear her? — to reproduce for you *the authoress's existence* — *the existence of authoress* — writing against a re*birth* — writing against predicates — refusing maintenance — an idiopathic familiar syndrome of whipped words, of gusts tearing the abnormal hemlock — high on the hill, a red-cunted imp under familiar mountain laurel — mourning doves moaning — greensprouted allele greeting pinkmelted spring — you sentenced to redheaded silence — the familial hemlock penned — redhairs to the breeze — verbs nowhere to be sought — a syntaxed agent — triple-tonguing triptolemus — proposing no progeny — adopting *only* the unparented — from which he was not his blood; she was not his blood; you will not be her blood —

unparenting ending the predicated sentence, the sentence predicated upon hemlock, the hemlock predicated on progeny, the progeny predicated on prose, prose predicated on predicates, predicates predicated on silence

Please explain what you have said about the subject.

Hey man, that Triptolemus shit, it's all Greek to me.

The norm lives quietly, without speaking.

Pardon me. You think you are finished, but I am not. She said.
Her family sentence finally diagrammed, she begins (*n.b.*: This would be Part Two) to collect photographs. It is the women who are impossible to track. "Anne Gettig," the caption reads. "Do not know her."
What is it she desires to go back to?

Since time is not time, it is simply change (see Chapter 5), so passed time is really passed change — so

¿Que pasa? Pero que será, será.

She stands at the worktable in Budget Framer. The beautiful Filipino woman takes her photo and measures it. "7 1/2," she scribbles on the order form. She squints in an attempt to interpret the sepiaed background. A rough-hewn fence — isn't that what a novelist would call it? — a syntax of the heart? — "rough-hewn"? — a roughly hewn fence stretches behind eight yellowed people gathered on chairs on — what? their lawn? — Thomas Fleisher rather ostentatiously in the center — as if he were more than

(sperm)

and do please note the subjective tense there — *as if*

plus, keep in mind, as perhaps you have not, that she has no [ ] ("nothing," she said, and hung up — "did you ever call her back?")

and she has no ("IS THIS YOUR SPERM?") children

"Maggie McClellan, believed to be daughter of Thomas F."

it is the closed-captioned women who are impossible to (verb-on-verb) hear

At Budget Framer she squints at the woman far more beautiful than she (Other woman) and commits a participle

"Myrtle Faust. Not known."

speaking of which, since we are apparently related, would she sell her soul to the devil for (choose one) 1) a [ ]; 2) a child; 3) a stunningly written sentence to be diagrammed and splayed across 4) the width of that rough-hewn fence like a Seneca blanket

they were farmers you know — the Seneca — the battles were so brutal because farmers fought farmers for rolling hills of hemlock

captions betray the captured

"Carrie Horner. Do not know."

what you do not know can obscure you

"Not known. A good guess might be Mary E. wife of Harry Fleisher."

and please do note the passive verb there, agentless — *who did not know her? who?? who meant the not-knowing???*

but it is the guessing game that plagues her and ultimately she stands in Budget Farmer (good typo, under the circumstances, will keep), Visa Debit Card in hand, bereft of credit, and she will be charged $89 for the privilege of hanging her family sentence diagrammed on a wall which will someday belong to

"It is excellent you wish for UV glass," Other says, "since of course you want to give to your children someday. You have not the original, no?"

the (ab)original what she knew to be the [ ]less childless WHERE THE FUCK IS THE SPERM and have you noticed that

women intellectuals and artists so often fail to reproduce at replacement levels

what he was saying

since, you know, he was obsessed with theory — a poet-theorist, she called him — obsessed with them all — risk theory, uncertainty theory, chaos theory, catastrophe theory (theory theory — ha!, he wrote in her margins)

captioned, as you were, not in *time* but in

(myth — Triptolemus, he be *myth*, man)

change now, please, i do not like you

no wait change the myth back

My *real* question is, *theoretically*, shouldn't the people who take the greatest risk with language reap the greatest *reward* for that risk? And if the answer is uncertain, do we not face catastrophe? Who will risk language if the reward be not naming?

The women wear lace. The men wear suits. Thomas wears a beard.

This is where you come from. A rough-hewn fence behind suitable great-great lace. The women, unrecorded.

It's worst when they don't marry. Can't find the unmanned anywhere.

Did you look over there?

Where at?

("we thought you'd be happier when you found a man")

Also when they do not have children — marrying and birthing being — well, I don't have to tell *you*.

What did they do for a living?

They cut down trees. Slaughtered sylvania. Hewed the hemlock. That was after the Seneca, of course.

And, as you know, some of my best friends are Native.

He is six-foot-six, tall as Pennsylvania corn, has always been handsome, and *that* has been the most regrettable thing about his destiny.

Where is *she*? "Nothing."

He stands by the tombstone. A palsy (idiopathic familiar syndrome, she has it too) causes the hand on his all-the-bells-and-whistles camera to shake. She argues with him about whether the "C" on "MACELLA" is really a "G." She is a language worker, so naturally she reaches her hand forward to feel the letter. A brown moss crumbles beneath her fingers. "I feel a spur," she says, fingering ancient stone. "It's a 'G.'"

"Huh," he says, his hands shaking as he advances the film. She falls to her knees, a language worker, copying the data into a notebook. "Magella. Pretty name."

This is where they come from. Six-foot-six and corn-handsome stands next to the stone with the marker left by the Daughters of the American

Evolution and she takes his picture, copies down the data into a notebook. This is chaos. This is where she comes from; this is the end of abstraction. Data accumulates; the dialogue is inane. "So he fought in the revolution?" "Might have." "Well, you know what that makes me then." "I do. But they're not sure — he may have only fought in the Indian wars." "Well, you know what that's make you then." "What's that."

Catastrophe in apostrophe: You know that poet-theory is unpredicated, right? Consider the humble spur. It takes so little to make a C unfamiliar. Just a little mark.

Also: They were Lutherans. This was long after they were no longer Jewish. They took the "C" out of their name so there would be no confusion — all should know, they were not chosen.

It was butchers they were.

"An Indian Killer, that's what."

Corn. Did someone mention corn? Triptolemus, you know, a man taught by a woman (well, both of them were myths, really — right?), to sow seeds. Corn seeds. *Maize.* How to spread, broadcast, manifest the destiny.

What was her name again?

Who?

Triptolemus's teacher?

Do not know her.

Later that night, they went outside and stood in the dark. They'd heard the space shuttle was going to fly over. Heads up: the sky was clear. Crystal clear. Back there. Back home.

When all else fails, deploy Visa.

The language worker diagrams the family sentence, frames the sepia tones of loss — or is it change — forks over the debit card for the future of no one, nothing. Unmanned, her pits shaved, her T's spurred, I dangle her modifiers, fight for her Englishes, place the predicates at the end of the sentence as tradition requires (the cunt over the fence some man throw) and consider the cremation of her typescripts. When you know you are dying, it is pleasant to control the end.

Riddle me this, hackman:

I have no mother and no children. What am I?

(Pardon me. I mean I have no [ ] and no children.)

Her name was Demeter. Her daughter was lost. She went looking for her.

(In Hades. But hey.)

Could not find her. Taught men to sow instead.

Rough-hewn, implacable, irreproducible, *implacable* ("look it up!") — fence, was it? — a change-link fence? — one plank was down, over there — when did they fix that? 1913? — fully diagrammed. The women wore lace. And yellowed. Became passively lost. Matted a deep olive green. Framed polished blood. She owns it, that spur. *SHH!!* An epic static heard only by the normatively hemlocked. Definitely an aboriginal, a keeper, since opposites do not attract men —

— the ideogrammatic familiar.

(End of Part DINK.)

8:
Honeymoon

So. There will be not. Back to. Two live steeped in dangling signifiers. To recap:

Scenario: two ladies who lunch. Your basic faux-urban restaurant, too small, too crowded, too pretentiously expensive. As before, the requisite mesclun greens. Lady A, eyes shining, face lifted to heaven, smugly content (so right away, you know she's the bad guy), puts down her fork. Says to Lady B (and I quote):

You just have no idea (her head shakes profoundly). When you have a child, you just have no idea the love you're capable of feeling. No idea. You'd never think it possible. It changes *everything*.

Enjambment being impossible in an age of unmetered parking verse, she could only know what side her breath was buttered on. And while we're on the subject, Barbiephiles, let me be perfectly clear (tho not the first to say it): I'll buy postfeminism when I'm sold on postpatriarch

Lace-light air settles. Pass the butter — it's not good for you — pass it I said — not so much! mind your own plate — you are my plate — and Ooooooh, they have an X down here! The idea you ignore is this one: that consonants and vowels equal call and response, especially for the heterosexually interactive.

Gusty winds may exist across the street and home becomes the trade wind — is it time to vacuum yet? I'll help, windbag — if we can dig the mold out of this window casing maybe your temperature will come down some. Hold your breath a long long time, since it's a long way to Hazard.

Today she died. He died tomorrow. He would have died today but he was waiting for beurre blanc. Transcendence, after all, is a fucklot of work. And she had been an interstate birder: what falcon? Over there! — look where I'm pointing! Where? Sitting on the fence post! You never look where I point.

At the next table, a member of the target world asks the waiter about an entry on the menu. "It's kind of a *deconstructed* paella," he regurgitates. In truth, a radish a day keeps the rales away, although I wonder — is there a difference between permanent vision and retina burn? Of course, this would be pastiche.

Who should go first, do you think? X? Y? I think I could handle it better than you. I have more steps. I know how to ask for ball-change. I trow. I make him look both ways, she said, when he bungee jumps. I mean, I assume you're childless because you're the feminist. Right? More cheese?

Encrypted in the postlanguage information age, consonants akimbo, they sat in booth 4. I'll have the happy family, wheezed the white woman. Eggrolls with that? gasped her Asian wife. There's no use crying over spilt logos, but the fact is, plot was too violent a device for you. Someone always had to sigh.

You have to promise me that if something just happened here you'll come and be with him. Ventilate. I have all the accounting stuff together in case something travels to the hitching post. You two times two. Zero before, zero after. Two to the second power. It's a long way to haggard.

You have no idea to the power of twenty, forty times less than hero. Spared, we were, the frightful hare — now exhale. Where? Take the word "feminism": a fricative, a sibilant, some mm-mmn-goods, and e-i-e-i — oh. The image t-r-e-e is not itself a chart of related people. Of stumpage we have aplenty.

His seatbelt was broken and she found the accounting stuff. $X = Y$ except when it doesn't, but you have no ideology. She's driving down the road and she can see it, the deer leaps out and she loses control, skids, hits the and you wake up right when it — you have to promise me. He's not. Sable.

What will it be like? She breathes in, exfoliates. There will be lace, the thought of smoked salmon in a roue, then there will not be. Will be, not be. To have and not to have, as the translation had it ill. It will arrive with the breath of a comma. With no waiting for a consonant to lean on, to free the breeze.

The host culture suppressed the outbreak populations, so we are compelled to admit — in a post-apocalyptic sense — that the rain forest is a great work of art. His Latin accent sucks, but there's no one to badger anyway. Writing as anthropogenic *terra preta* — think about it. Constant resowing of fertile microbes.

Of course I will want you there, she said, when I go-go, another aerobic activity, would not want you to find me skating, would want you to wait though. What we're really after here is the thickness of the line — are we there yet? Husband was first a verb, you know, which means something.

If it's you first, I would keen, and you would end up feeling feathered for me and you would not get to enjoy. You have no idea and you never point up the possible. It's advanced. It's difficult. It is not for the heart-smart ass. It is easier to pester a broodilence, trust me. *Femme* — an ism unhusbanded.

Since there is no front ranging, you can sprinkle me off Pole Steeple, near South Mountain, 3 over from Tuscarora — Norm will spill into the Juniata from Jack's Mountain, 2 the other way — as for you, I'd sprinkle you youknowwhere but I know you and snow and I know how you'd gasp and caw.

[Start next book here.] Since two inelastic *isolatos* equals one *desaparacido*. Here now, long forever, geometric structures failing — not one, not two, not three. A = you, B = me; us as hypotenuse. Whichever Pythagorean goes last, don't forget to turn off the lights — what, were you born in a Potterybarn?

No, it won't be a grand leap but really rather the opposite of X, it will be the fullness of empty, don't you see, the impossibly loved there-not, you don't have to be there but you have to help me hear it — and you have — know ideal — how much you will — X will — not being equal after all this.

She died two weeks after him, you know, I never forgave her, but she said I'm not needed anymore and they sprinkled her in the gulf, redundant perhaps, on the other side of the abyss. I never missed a day of tool. She said. For symbolic utility purposes, the vowel launched from the consonant.

The portal's coil called and you had no ideals. How inflated. It is a kiss on satin belly. I wouldn't fight with anyone but you. I lunch on these people and you are still my favorite silken breast, sweet-and-sour ear, swallow toes. For our last supper I shall serve you nothing possible.

Us to the second degree, us and then some, what we did for, what combatants we, how wounded that day the woman said you were trying to keep me from expressing my — a formidable double, he said that day at Pastabilities but he didn't know the half of — excuse me whilst I excommunicate.

As consumption manager she selected the fertility procedures, and choosy mothers choose IUIs. Their doomsday clock ticking, they ride without rein, celebrate Dia de los Muertos, crunch sugar skulls between their teeth, revise free wills, resee skeletons as artwork, reach for the contrail of the shuttle.

In the absence of triangulars, what's possible is an improvised binary. Poem meets prose meets Mr. X, and why? Mistakes were made in the excision, in the exhalation, the wind tunnel. It's been an excellent week for balding eagles. One off the seatbuckled interstate, one in empty skylight, one in a pair.

Pass the Y, would you, since what I say creates a repeatable sequence but one so complex that you can't possibly understand, translation being susceptible to decay and you being a poet and all. I was once a pregnant thing, a revision in progress, breathing water — was it gills? But I repeat myself.

After all, brined placentas are more tender — but no more butter, dammit — did you hear the crematorium burned down? Ashes to ashes times two all over again and in dusty circumstances we mask inhalation — I've scold you and scold you, Y starts with the left foot, Xing the right. Ain't I a image?

Aging (she joked) is not for the squamous. Pythagoras (recalls the poet) speculated that humans die because they cannot rejoin their beginnings to their ends, cannot close the circle, cannot connect the dotted hypotenuse. Her especially, given inelastic ova. She loves his name, more vowel than consonant.

If it all ended yesterday, I've had a good deal of lace and sage, a soupçon of tarragon too, and tenses incorrect, but the syntax of the dance should be symmetrical — you come, you snow, you choose, you deal, and if my fever's cooler tomorrow we'll go into town and look for X to rebut your Y.

Never miss a day. Understand your process, avoid your normish-mennonite fears, carpe scheming, know your simulations. A day without rationalization is like a day without Y not. Lay lady — say, come here often? You have no idea how much you love when it is just you through. To the mat. No static.

I know enough to lance to dance, kick the tireds, step slightly but always carry a big leftist. You, I don't know about. I fear you after. Love an infinitesimal vocabulary. Forty fucking words for blow but when twenty old joyfreinds find me going down on pixels, it's you I need to teach me satin.

Give her a lyric and she takes a mile, he complained. It's me you hosed, it's you just us. And you have no idea. The defendence. Of justness. The digestibilities, linguistic entropy being decomposition of communication, communication decomposition of breath, breath resurrection of vowels.

You pick up after me. I read your decay. Opposition affirmation and up next, a progressive two-step following an east-west swing. The innerstater perches on the lamppost, well ventilated, warble lost in translation. Just we two. Take a breath. That's what it will be — a breath here, then not there.

Find freedom: fold the love over and over. Roll the dough, place the butter in the center, and fold the dough over twice. Roll, fold, turn, watch the butter spread against every layer, later to lift the elastic whilst escaping, evaporating. Turns: two plus two plus two equals 12 puffs of steam.

X taught Y to scatter seeds, X being an asthmatic diastemic, Y being merely asthmatic. I inhale he exhales. I catch his breath. The proesie lives in the vowel, how many times do I have to tell you this most impossible idea. Love, dearest — love the vowel. She is your interself in a nest of ifs.

So if we are postfeminism (as if), postmodernism (big if), postlanguage (if how), we must then post the past to a community site (seems clear enough). Thus pastiche of this sort, prose with poem, past-proem, impossibly if-less, impossible soft-butter pastry. That language stuff — too easy to be hard. Said he.

With shared food, there is no mine about it. My butter, your bread. In my recumbency, she awaits the sternutation, full of bereavement in their breath to feel. We are condemned to prose poems because readers have revoked the poetic sentence. No time left for seeding. Only reason.

"Squamous. S-Q-U-A-M-O-U-S. adj. Scaly, therefore quickly reproducing." The two of them, 2 x 2 x 2, 2 cubed, eight letters home, half vowels half consonants. He is more breath than resistance, but more love than breath. She remembers what he'll do tomorrow, unsentenced brilliance.

Intertwined, he the poem (natch), she the prose, they suffer freedom to assemble. Say a proem when you can't breathe — ass-pro-em-bled. Fuck the ass, of course — who needs it. I can't possibly remember when you will go — hence, we will rant unheard about the scenic of beauty.

Pardon my Franktitude — they don't pronounce their consonants anyway, so who can say. I chain the vowel to breath, the eagle runflies, she chases the gales, brings me no roue, no fucking fricative, and postpatriarchy, darling, will arrive postrace and not a moment before. Now exhale. I shall say I no more.

In the belly of love lies bread, an uncertain relation of opposition because I could not rise for breath. The hinge to life. I will stroke. In the end there will be only hands. Yours, mine, hours. Two hands. Two fingers breathing, until one will inhale and the other will exhale, and that will be all she wrote.

The satin belly, the thing that exhumes his back, the Avon'd, beadless gown of kin, the defiant oneness defined by beurre rouge vowels, in the bosom buried, verbless, husbanded. Who should first? An impossible tenth-hour idea, as there is no knowing between she and she, vowels lost in rattle.

Breathing hands, and you can't possibly know about time — that hinge being, after all, an interrupted sentence. Whichever I imagined, whichever interrupted, no mine about it, and forgive me for not ending in modernism — better still, for not signifying. She assembles opposition, after all. It's satin he feels.

The preceding contains samples from:

Joe Amato

Jane Austen

Samuel Beckett

Charlotte Brontë

Emily Brontë

Raymond Carver

Sharon Doubiago

Raymond Federman

Lyn Hejinian

Susan Howe

Steve Katz

Audre Lord

Carole Maso

Harryette Mullen

Laura Mullen

William Shakespeare

Juliana Spahr

Gertrude Stein

Laurence Sterne

Ronald Sukenick

Sojourner Truth

Anne Waldman

about the author

Kass Fleisher is the author of *The Bear River Massacre and the Making of History* (SUNY Press, 2004). She teaches at Illinois State University in Normal.

recent and new books from chax press

Tenney Nathanson, *Erased Art* (New West Classics 5)

Heather Nagami, *Hostile*

Caroline Koebel and Kyle Schlesinger, *Berlin Schablone*

Linh Dinh, *American Tatts*

Patrick Pritchett, *Burn: Doxology for Joan of Arc*

Jonathan Brannen, *Deaccessioned Landscapes*

David McAleavey, *Huge Haiku*

Norman Fischer, *Slowly but Dearly*

Keith Wilson, *Transcendental Studies* (New West Classics 4)

Beverly Dahlen, *A-Reading Spicer & 18 Sonnets* (New West Classics 3)

David Bromige, *As in T As in Tether* (New West Classics 2)

Nathaniel Tarn, *The Architextures* (New West Classics 1)

Nick Piombino, *Hegelian Honeymoon*

Jerome Rothenberg, *A Book of Concealments*

Bill Lavender, *While Sleeping*

Elizabeth Treadwell, *Chantry*

Allison Cobb, *Born Two*

Todd Baron, *TV Eye*

Karen Mac Cormack, *Implexures*

Pierre Bettencourt, *Fables*

Heather Thomas, *Resurrection Papers*

Nathaniel Mackey, *Four for Glenn*

Charles Bernstein, *Let's Just Say*

Hank Lazer, *Deathwatch for My Father*

Mark Weiss, *Figures: 32 Poems*

For additional titles please visit our web site: http://www.chax.org/

This and other projects by Chax Press are supported by the Tucson
Pima Arts Council and by the Arizona Commission on the Arts with
funding from the State of Arizona and the National Endowment for
the Arts.

Arizona
Commission
on the Arts

NATIONAL
ENDOWMENT
FOR THE ARTS